THE PHANTOM'S TEA

THE PHANTOM'S TEA

THE STARE

...a paranormal investigation
and a hydro-galactic war

DANICA MENDEZ

Dedicated to the Legion of Venom

...let's keep this best-seller ride going...

...thanks for the stares...

THE PHANTOM'S TEA

The Phantom's Tea
There's a place in the darkness
It shouldn't involve me
But I know if you go there
You'll hear the Phantom's Tea
With every sip the Phantom takes
He gives you quite a tale
Alone and scared you'll soon become
This happens without fail
So listen at your own risk
Be careful what you do
Join his table if you dare
But the tea will soon star you

CONTENTS

The Phantom's Tea Table: Behind the Tea!

PARANORMAL INVESTIGATION REPORT: S

Location: Well...I'm still here in this ancient cave. However, now I am resting under the illumination of mystical paranormal writing.

Date: October 1st

Time: Midnight

Notes:

Air bubbles began to frantically surround me, each carrying the last few breaths of air I would ever take. My eyes were fused shut. Any time I tried to open them, the harsh stings of salt water felt like my eyes would be sealed shut forever. Thrashing around aimlessly was all I could do. But the more I flailed around, the more difficult it became to catch my breath.

Yellow. No, not just yellow. Gold. My eyes became acquainted with the visions of shimmery gold starlight thrashing in chaos. A tornado of gilded shooting stars left me both confused and mesmerized. Through the lustrous waves I could see a great beast swimming all around me. The waves the monster left behind rocked my body back and forth in its tide. Was I in danger? I darted backwards. I needed one more look. I wondered if maybe what I was seeing was simply an effect of salt water in my eyes? Maybe it was the fact that I was losing oxygen fast? But that wasn't the case. I saw pure magic. I saw...a living legend.

I'm safe now, but sleeping is *not* an option! A few moments ago, I decided to just... *rest*... my eyes for a moment, but I became restless due to the neon green glow from the cave's ancient hieroglyphics. My eyes and my brain are truly...haunted. I couldn't keep my eyes closed! Images of glowing maritime civilizations painted long-lost stories across the cave's ceiling. I studied them for hours! I wondered if I had the only set of eyes ever to witness this artifact? Was this the greatest story...never...told? That's the thing about artifacts of the past. You never know the full stories they hold. There are entire periods of history that we will just...never truly uncover. It's crazy to think that facts of the past can be changed simply by the passing of time and uninformed mouths retelling stories that gradually paint nothing into something...or something into...nothing.

Studying the hieroglyphics, I could tell one thing for sure: Once upon a time, an ancient seaside village existed. The hieroglyphics painted stories of fish markets, boating industry, and agriculture by the sea. I could see depictions of people trading fish, tending to crops, bustling around the crowded community looking busy. I know the exact ancient civilization the picture is portraying. Legend has it...or...history *had* it...that this community was plagued with a great curse. Apparently the villages were haunted by a certain evil entity that would keep a close eye on everything and everyone. The villagers would always feel a looming, eerie sense that someone was watching them at all times. It was said that if you did something the prying eye considered wrong, you vanished without a trace. How unfair is that? Imagine someone's opinion of you dictating whether you stay or disappear into eternal mystery!

Anyway, there is an old tale of a young girl who decided to ignore her curfew and go to the river instead. As she made her way to the water, she danced excitedly and laughed her way to the river. When the young girl finally reached, she walked right up to the water to catch a glimpse of her reflection...but...it was not her staring back. Instead, the girl saw two massive glowing eyes of green staring back at her! The eyes looked like bottomless cosmic blackholes! The sinister, flashing lights of the stare made the young girl dizzy, and she fell into the river. After that, she was never seen again. The phantom stare would haunt the ancient village for the rest of time...or so they say. Eventually, all the villagers decided to move away in fear. No one could bear the haunting and looming paranoia created by this phantom gaze!

Deciding to inspect the hieroglyphics further, I moved in for a closer look. My nose was practically touching the ancient paintings while my eyes desperately searched for some sort of understanding of the people who once lived, perhaps exactly where I stood. I looked closely at the sea. With enormous wings, a body decorated in blades, and a vicious looking face featuring only one eye, I saw the great sea condor etched into history.

Maybe one eye is all he needed to see every single thing in the world and beyond?

The mythical sea condor. Magic. A once living legend. Part whale, part dragon, part bird. I guess? A brilliant sea monster with an equally powerful legend to match! Gliding through oceans of stars and dodging asteroids, the great sea condor dwelled in a part of the galaxy our eyes can't reach.

Legend has it that sea condors are the strongest creatures in existence. Their force and enormity made it impossible for them to dwell here on Earth as no location could handle their mesmerizing mass and might. That's why sea condors once lived in the sky amongst the stars. In the galactic world, the great beasts have all the space they need to thrive.

Why are they now in our seas, you might ask? The ancient myth tells of a great war that broke out in the hydro-galaxy that resulted in all sea condors being banished to the depths of the sea for all eternity. You can find them now nestled deep within the ocean unknown...so they say...

Let's go back to the details! The sea condor is massive...I mean ginormous! Imagine an airplane that's very much alive, heartbeat and all. The great monster's body is covered in metallic blades that resemble majestic swords, and his wingspan is as dramatic as a jet plane. With every move of his bladed wings, an enormous glowing sea wind causes wild riptides and underwater tornadoes, throwing fish and other sea creatures in every direction! These hydro-galactic predators soar through the great sea cutting through winding currents like a great machete cutting through overgrown terrain in an underwater rainforest! Perhaps the most shocking aspect of the sea condor's appearance is their one eye, but I will report more on that finding a little later. First, I need to explain more about this ancient picture!

In the far corner of the ancient hieroglyphics, I could see crop circles surrounded by meadows of Dracula orchids, which are pretty creepy in their own right. These bold blossoms boast a center that looks like a face... almost as if they are living! They say when you lock eyes with a Dracula orchid's "eyes," no matter which direction you move, their stare will follow you.

Opposite the orchids was the island and the cave where I stand in this present moment. It's clear there is a mystery to be solved, and I am standing center stage. By the way, I haven't mustered the courage to open this phantom book. I'm still...just...a little freaked out by it! Why was this ancient relic so protected? I'll find out tomorrow as I open the book when the clock strikes 3:33 at twilight. After all, that's what Cal said I had to do. I'm off for now!

Phoenix

PARANORMAL INVESTIGATION REPORT: V

Location: Out at sea

Date: October 3rd

Time: 4:44 AM

Notes:

Tonight was rough. It was 3:22 in the morning, and for some reason, there was not one star in the sky. I decided to take out the old row boat I found to complete my first mission. For some reason, I felt like opening the book was safer at sea than on land!

The ocean was beautiful tonight. The waves sparkled with phytoplankton that looked like aquatic shooting stars glowing confidently despite the depth and mystery of the sea. Gentle waves of bioluminescent water sparkled as if concealing hidden treasures of the world underneath. The phytoplankton illuminated the sea, creating a galaxy of underwater enchantment that simply took my breath away. I was watching the renegade light of the phytoplankton paving a brilliant emerald path to the edge of the earth. The shimmering waves cut the black sky like a blade, proving that the sea holds more secrets and light than the effervescent mystery behind the stars. With every move of my oar, the lights beyond the sea twinkled gloriously. It was as if I was mixing a magical potion with every brush my oar took.

The war between the deep darkness of the night sky and the sharp shine of the luminescent waves made me think about the cursed sea condors. Perhaps the answers were...in the book. Now was the time.

My eyes couldn't help but analyze the cover. The wrinkles from the old leather paved paranormal roads where suppleness once lived. My fingers began to trace a path of deep etching that only time could have created on this once beautiful book. I was entranced! The cracks of time painted scenes and images—they reminded me of those that appeared in the wooden doors outside the forbidden classrooms at my old boarding school. See...that legend was true. If you looked closely at the woodwork of the older classrooms, you could see tiny depictions of scenes and characters. Some kids at school thought it was all fake, that if you saw something, you surely were making something out of nothing! I just...couldn't stop thinking about the ancient book. The haunting hieroglyphics on the cover depict a vile beast with horrific detail! I've never seen anything like this monster before...or have I? Is it the same creature that tried to maul me and protect this very book? Looking at the cover more closely, I can see a tiny message inscribed above the creature that reads, "...truth or dare." My "friend," Cal told me that in order to complete the dare, I must rip a random page out of this book, make it into a paper airplane and fly it at exactly 3:33 in the morning.. Oh...and I was not allowed to read the page or else the dare doesn't count!

My fingers confidently slipped to the middle of the book and gripped a page. I tightened my grip, swiftly ripped out the page, and instantly collapsed.

The pain was unbearable—it felt like my hand had been chopped off! Frigid blood began to drip from my hand and down my arm. I screamed in agony! Suddenly, I managed to whip my head upward. Standing right over me was some sort of ghost! His blood-red ocean eyes met mine and his calculated but gentle smile seemed amused! His pale, almost shining skin was like a phantom mirror, and I saw my own reflection starting back! I noticed that dark shadows had replaced my eyes. I was dying...or worse... transforming into some sort of heinous monster. Somehow, I mustered the strength to stand up and start swinging my arms wildly toward the mirror. The apparition faded slowly. I quickly looked down to check my hand.

There was a thin river of blood traveling from the tip of my finger and down my wrist. It didn't look like a big deal, but the pain was excruciating. A paper cut? That's it?

I remember the steps Cal gave me for folding a paper airplane. I replayed his words in my head: "Turn the page around. Fold the paper in half, then take the two upper edges and fold them into triangles. Reinforce the crease a couple times. Fold two outside edges on either side."

I made the airplane but I couldn't shake the curiosity of what was on the page! It was now or never. I threw the plane straight ahead and let it fly. It went quite a long distance; I squinted my eyes and saw a tiny beam of light illuminating from the delicate aircraft. What the...? The plane waned and wobbled then began to descend about twenty yards ahead of me. As I ran to catch up, the mysterious light began to flicker. I stopped dead in my tracks. The plane floated above my head, perhaps looking for a safe place to land, and as it hovered I could see the details. The paper had tiny wrinkles that looked like cracks made from turbulent weather. I couldn't believe my eyes. What was I waiting for? The plane was close enough for me to grab! With great courage and curiosity, I thrusted my hand up toward the airplane. I struck like lightning, snatching it right out of the luminescent sky!

Now this little paper airplane was just a crumpled piece of paper inside my clenched fist.

I slowly opened up the crumpled mess one fold at a time as if it was made of delicate glass. Piece by piece, edge by edge, my fingers carefully performing surgery. Finally, I could see the mystery message! The paper read:

"Turn around before you're dead
This message is best left unread
Your dare is here, it's a twist of fate
Open that box, you'll find the number eight
Give it a shake before you go
There's so much more you need to know
Turn around"

My neck began to tense up as I cautiously turned my head. Who...or what...was behind me. I was being watched. Suddenly, the light of the waves ceased and I couldn't see anything—until a wild herd of lightning bugs swarmed me! The light of their tails tingled my skin with a calming warmth. But then the peaceful warmth became a painful scalding on my skin, and their bright light began to blind me. I struggled to shake the bugs off and eventually fell to my knees. The lightning bugs covered every inch of my skin. Their light began to evaporate the tears on my face. Suddenly...all at once...the bugs extinguished their light. My skin instantly cooled off. I had to keep going.

I decided to paddle back to the cave where I am now hoping to sleep this off! The mystery continues! If I had a phytoplankton for every question still lingering in my head, I could light up an entire galaxy. Will report more tomorrow...if I even make it through the night.

Phoenix

PARANORMAL INVESTIGATION REPORT: E.2

Location: A bed of phantom venom

Date: October 4th

Time: dawn

Notes:

This morning— I woke up covered in...phantom venom. This stuff is not your typical snake venom; it's supernatural. Phantom venom is puke green, fluorescent, and has the consistency of slimy, thick webs of poison. As I laid there stuck, scared, and disgusted, I took a closer look at the vile venom and saw the remnants of dead bugs! A goopy graveyard river of broken wings, fractured tails, floating pincers, bug guts and eyeballs covered my body from head to toe. I couldn't move a muscle.

The story behind phantom venom is a curious one. Legend has it that phantom venom comes from the unknown galaxies beyond the stars we can identify. The most chilling fact about this venom is that it has an actual pulse and mind of its own!

At night, the venom makes its way through our stratosphere and attacks anyone who gets too curious on their quest to discover the secrets of the sea and stars. Some say the venom can kill you. Some say the venom can turn you into some sort of phantom. Some even say the venom can take one of your eyes away by engulfing your face and melting one right off. I knew the risk of coming out here, but this is the mission I vowed to take! I accepted the dare, after all!

As I laid still, the phantom venom began making its way to my face. I knew that if it got into my ears, the vicious venom would potentially seep into my brain! Imagine a slime of dead bugs taking over your brain?! As the venom got closer and closer, two claws gripped into my right shoulder, causing a river of cold blood to stream down my arm. The claws belonged to some kind of creature that began to howl and bark with terrifying echoes unknown to my ears. Though my ears knew I was in trouble, my eyes still could not get a good look at who...or...what... was attacking me. Fighting off this mystery beast while trying to loosen the grip of the phantom venom was nearly impossible. Once I finally broke my arms free of the venom's chain-like hold, the monster opened my arms and handed me a strange object as he ran off. From what I could see through my own tears and drops of phantom venom in my eyes, the monster was absolutely enormous! His fur was a filthy, dusty looking blue and his hands appeared to be... webbed...but with giant claws. Was he from the sea? His slimy fins created a path around his head, across his arms, and down his spine. What mesmerized me the most was the beast's tail. His tail had a blazing, blue fire hovering over it. The wild lightning blue flashes and flames captivated every bit of my attention. Everyone knows that a blue flame is the hottest flame on Earth! Something just did not add up. Why is this sinister savage handing me something rather than disintegrating me with his blue flame tail of doom? Wild animals hunt to kill, not to...give gifts. As I noticed that the creature was running away, I decided to get brave. "Stop! Don't take another step!" I yelled. The beast stopped dead in his tracks. His spine of fins contorted and twitched in frustration as he began to turn around...slowly. I got a glimpse of his strong wolf ears. I was dealing with some sort of werewolf...but...he also had slimy fins up and down his spine? I leapt to my feet and got into a defensive stance. With every ounce of courage left, I said, "...not another move." Finally, the creature revealed his face. One...yes...I said ...ONE eye glistened in the moonlight from the cracks of the cave's ceiling. The beast opened his mouth to reveal his giant fangs, but the shadows continued to conceal most of the gruesome details of his appearance. I stood there, shivering in fear, but overwhelmed with questions and curiosity.

I took a few brave steps forward when I realized what was in my hand. The beast had given me a...a...magic eight ball.

PARANORMAL INVESTIGATION REPORT:N

Location: the haunted bridge

Date: October 5th

Time: unknown

Notes:

A deep chill built a frozen cage around my hands. My bones somehow felt like fragile icicles and scorching flames at the same time. Every breath I took turned to vapor in the air and clouded my vision. Winter fell upon me...somehow. My teeth began to chatter. In the distance, I could see the great beast. Once the fog of my own breath lifted, I could see the monster staring me down with his cyclops eye.

I looked down at my feet to make sure they were not frozen blocks of ice. The magic eight ball rested gently above my shoelaces. I picked it up. Instead of the typical cloudy blue water inside the magic eight ball, it appeared to contain some sort of deep red liquid. Almost like...blood. I began to give it a shake to reveal some sort of message. Suddenly, the eight ball's window revealed what looked to be a human eyeball! I freaked out and dropped it as I fell backwards in fright. Once the ball hit the ground, I could have sworn I saw the eye blinking! I screamed in terror and pulled myself back on my feet. Collecting my thoughts and catching my breath, I began to convince myself that I was imagining things! I was being silly, letting my paranoia of the paranormal get the best of me? I decided to give it one more shot.

I slowly walked back towards the eight ball, this time marching to loud drumbeats of my nervous heart. I picked the ball up and decided to ask a question. "Magic eight ball, why am I here?" I asked with a fake confidence as if I wasn't scared for my life. I shook the ball once more and waited for a message to appear. This time, the window showed me what looked like a tiny hurricane of red sweeping through the inside of the ball. I saw worms, spiders, and other bugs fill the window, but it didn't phase me. Anything was better than an eyeball. Abruptly, the storm of blood and worms stopped and a message appeared.

"Run."

I violently whipped my body around, causing the paranormal magic eight ball to slip from my hands and crack into one million pieces on the ground! The crash sounded like an orchestra of evil, shrieking instruments shattering through haunted stained-glass windows. I stopped dead in my tracks and looked down. I couldn't believe my eyes! Suddenly a river of red blood rushed around me! Was this what was inside the magic eight ball of doom? A ferocious stream of blinking eyeballs, green spiders, and bloodworms filled the phantom river! The tide was rising fast!

I tried everything I could to run away, but beneath the garish river of blood there seemed to be some kind of phantom venom quicksand! I screamed for help! Suddenly the beast lunged on me from across the crimson river! Next thing I knew I was hoisted out of the river and on to the beast's back. He began swimming frantically, but the current was viciously strong!

I could feel the worms slither into my

socks and shoes. I felt the eyeballs making their way into my pockets and socks! The horror! Next thing I knew... everything went blank.

I woke up to the sounds of my body getting dragged on the dusty cave ground. Particles and debris blinded my vision and filled my mouth. I couldn't see anything...nothing...but I could feel a cold, sharp grip on my wrist!

I tried to flip over to get a good look at who had such a gruesome grip on me. With every move I made, the beast grew more frustrated! I began to scream for help!

Finally, we came to a stop. I shot up onto my feet and immediately put my hands up. I was ready to fight for my life but I couldn't see anything standing in front of me! How could I possibly protect myself? Who was I even fighting? That's when some sort of switch went off.

One neon light appeared beyond the shadows and showed me everything I needed to see. One. Blue. Flame. It was the beast and his flame tale. The scorching electric blue had the magnitude of a small forest fire. Completely dynamic, ever-changing with different shades of blue, I was under a spell of curiosity once again! The animal was holding the ancient book from earlier, and a mysterious spray can aimed right at my face. His one eye held me in a gripping gaze that chilled me to the bone. I could not believe his...stare. The beast's entire face was practically his one eye! His look was menacing yet majestic. Was he a friend or foe? The truth is...he saved my life. I took one step forward. Within a second, the beast pulled the trigger on the spraycan and unleashed some mysterious fog in my face! I began to cough wildly as I was engulfed! After stammering around the chilling cloud for a moment, I decided to stand still and cover my face. In a flash, the fog had lifted. I looked up to see the beast spray painting above him. As the fog lifted further, our setting was revealed! We were standing underneath a small bridge right beside the lake. Whatever was in the can was illuminating a secret message inscribed on the ceiling of the bridge. I slowly approached the monster, who seemed calm but hyper focused. I stood beside him, when suddenly he took the ancient book and flung it behind us! The book slammed to the ground and caused an enormous flash of blinding golden light! Hundreds of alphabets of golden letters began to jump off the ripped pages and float in the air, creating roads of sentences. The beast stopped and pointed to what the letters were writing. Here is what they said:

The Legend of The Stare

Millions of years ago, the world was caught in the middle of a constant war between the mysterious galaxies beyond the stars and the hidden depths of the enchanted sea. Humans walked the land in between, unaware that such empires existed above and below their own. The galactic kingdoms were wealthy and powerful, led by the fearsome Seyfert the Spinner of Darkness and the Legion of Venom. Leader Seyfert was known for his cunning personality and wicked ways. But physically, he was nothing more than a haunted skeleton...a somebody of time's past, who became a nobody because of his cruel ways. His garish face was a crude arrangement of bones...with a twist: His eye sockets glowed with a hauntingly bright neon green. Everyone in the Legion of Venom had the same eyes; they were all cursed because of...the stare. You see, Seyfert the Spinner of Darkness had once gotten himself into some trouble. His greed always led him by the nose. All he ever wanted was to be rich and powerful, ruler of the sky. One night, he decided to visit the old castle of the ancient emperor of the night sky. The emperor ruled all constellations, galaxies, stars, and though he despised company, he loved entertainment. So, the ruler decided to listen to Seyfert.

Seyfert knelt down to the emperor and

started to cry. "I just want a kingdom for myself," he wailed. "I want to be a leader, but nobody will listen to me! I would do anything to have power like yours, emperor, please make me like you! I'll do anything!"

The emperor looked to Seyfert with a devilish grin and said, "...anything?"

Seyfert stood up and shook the emperor's hand. The great leader took hold of Seyfert and threw him on his throne. Still holding onto the handshake with a vice-like grip, the emperor slid a gold and emerald ring on Seyfert's finger. He then lifted his hands to the sky and placed a spell on Seyfert. "I grant you...the ability to lead. You are a king now! But there is a catch: You will only lead with your greatest quality. If you have a good heart, you will lead with love; if you have a good mind, you will lead with intelligence. Only you know your main power, Seyfert. One more thing! If I am giving you a corner of my kingdom to lead, you will forever owe me the favor. I can come back at any time and take your power away with this one code."

"What's the code, your majesty?," Seyfert asked.

"I will not tell you or anyone else. I will hide the code within the stars where nobody but myself can find it. Now, the deal is done. Here is the key to your kingdom." The emperor turned on his heels and vanished into the darkness. Seyfert cried with joy! He was finally all he ever wanted to be...a leader. People would HAVE to listen to him now...or else. Seyfert ran over to the mirror in the corner of the emperor's quarters. He gazed upon his reflection but noticed something was quite different. Seyfert now had a green halo around his eyes. He brushed it off until one frightening thought entered his mind. His leading power... Was it greed? Was that why his eyes were green with envy? Seyfert couldn't turn back now, he had just made a deal. For the better, he hoped.

Storming out of the castle, Seyfert went on to rule his land for centuries. He drafted an army of his own by staring deep within the eyes of citizens and casting an evil spell that turned them into cold-blooded followers. His Legion of Venom led with greed, jealousy, and malice. Like a wicked contagion, Seyfert and his army cursed anyone who would gaze upon their stare. Their toxicity built an empire of its own. One day, the Legion of Venom asked Seyfert what his formal title should be.

"My name is Seyfert the Spinner of Darkness. I could convince anyone of anything and get what I want by controlling anyone I need to."

Seyfert did just that. He was able to lie, convince, and manipulate townspeople in a casually cruel way. Soon, strong webs of gray deceit began to overtake his empire, and in a matter of time, everything was covered. Seyfert didn't mind, for they were the webs he weaved, after all. One day, Seyfert and his Legion decided to go to the Eridanus river. Eridanus is a constellation that those on Earth can see in the night sky...even today. The great leader wanted to expand his empire and take over the land beneath the river. However, since the dawn of time, the river had been filled with mythical sea condors. The sea condors were brilliant and peaceful. As they swam throughout the river, a striking glow would shine through the currents and illuminate the rushing water like a glowing planet of its own. The Spinner of Darkness couldn't stand the sight of something shining that wasn't a product of his own doing. And so, he vowed to destroy all life below the surface of Eridanus!

At exactly 3:33 a.m. one brisk morning, the Legion of Venom arrived at Eridanus to bait the sea condors with galactic foods from their kingdom. As the food landed on the surface of the water, the sea condors watched from below. The snacks appeared like twinkling shooting stars reflecting the luminescent surface, appearing like tempting fireworks ready to be snatched! Slowly, the sea condors made their way to the surface. They couldn't resist the warm and energetic light of the bait. Neon reds, blues, and pinks colored the Eridanus river like fireworks on a glorious holiday. Almost every single sea condor came to the surface to celebrate! They swam and thrashed with contagious excitement...until they caught the stare of something sinister. Suddenly, the left eye of every condo vanished into thin air.

At the surface, the Legion took position. They gripped the ground tightly and focused their glare at the river. You see, Seyfert and the Venoms had one deadly power: They all possessed a stare that could freeze time and take lives. With one glance at this stare, you would feel your soul drain out of your body and through your feet. You won't remember who you were, what you loved, what you stood for, nothing is left. A person's individuality is completely erased and all thoughts are replaced with the opinions of the Legion of Venom. If they could lock eyes with the sea condors, they could make them vanish beyond the cosmos forever. One by one the sea condors would fall into the trap, and one by one they would disappear for eternity. One little sea condor named Sansu saw what was going on. He tried to warn his fellow tribe to avoid the hypnotizing fireworks that would eventually lead to the deadly glare. He swam wildly around his village, but his efforts were no match for the allure. Everyone took the bait, and suddenly a glimmer caught his own eye. Swimming slowly towards the surface, Sansu could not withstand the magical pull to follow the hallowed fireworks. His eyes began to grow with wonderment as he got closer and closer. Instantly, the sea was raining fireworks of terror. Chaos reigned as fireballs of fury began shooting through the galactic water. The sea condors swam for their lives! Only once before has anyone ever seen fire underwater.

A dizzying tide disoriented Sansu. He was no longer hypnotized. The great beast, leader of the underwater caves, saved Sansu. The warrior monster had a strong body of midnight blue fur, great blades as claws solid on his webbed hands, razor teeth, metallic fins up and down his spine, one eye, and a blue flame tale that radiated electric heat! His name was Cipher, short for Decipher. Cipher lived in the hydro-galactic river for centuries, protecting the sea condors and all that lived below the river. When the flames began shooting through the river, Cipher used his flame tale to herd Sansu and other sea condors to his cave to take shelter from the Legion. About twenty five sea condors made it into the cave to seek refuge from the firework war. The next morning, nearly everything and everyone had vanished.

Sansu searched feverishly for his family, but it was clear they had been banished. The sea condors cried out to their pods with haunting songs of longing and fear. Nobody answered. Cipher saw the destruction around him and knew exactly what he needed to do.

Cipher knew Seyfert and the Legion of Venom were greedy and wanted to lay claim to the river in order to control those who fell victim to the spell of the stare. He had to take the survivors somewhere safe. Cipher took out his powerful ancient book that was filled with old maps and folklore. Suddenly, Cipher knew where they needed to go. He told Sansu, "We will go to the land beneath the rock. That way, there is an entire world separating us from the stars. The land in between will stand in front of us, making it impossible for the galactic villains to disturb our peace. We must go to the sea but first, I need to take one of your eyes. For the curse of the stare only works on those with two eyes." Cipher grabbed his flame tail and shot into the sky, leaving behind a massive blue flash that filled the atmosphere. Every sea condor lost one eye that day, however, the banished eyes peacefully floated to the sky, becoming peaceful stars watching from above. Soon after Cipher sprung into action that day, the sea condors began to fill the world's oceans that still remain to this very day. Sea condors are now found in the far reaches of the seas, where no man could ever reach. These sea dragons don't want to be found. The further they are beneath the surface, the further they are from the stars. And so, the great beasts live in harmony scouring the ocean depths with one eye, longing to go back to their true home nestled within the star river.

————

I looked at the beast. One single tear fell from his cyclops eye. I was standing in front of the legendary Cipher. He closed the book abruptly and all the golden letters from the legend faded, revealing something else on the bridge. A neon red message beamed in our faces. It read:

The code is behind the Dracula Orchids

I think we need a recap!

List of Things I Know but Don't Want to Know but Still Need to Know

1. There is something called a sea condor...and we have not learned about them in Science class.
2. The sea condor has something to do with some ancient history
3. There is a werewolf/ vampire/ sea creature/ cyclops standing right next to me...and he really wants this creepy book.
4. This creepy book was found inside an old classroom at my school.

5. I'm a fool for taking this dare.

6. What are these Dracula orchids?

7. Who lives beyond them?

...this list of things I know has become a list of things I don't know!

Here is what I know for sure. The beast is Cipher. We both want to solve the code so he can go back home and...so can I. We're on the same page...the same team...I guess. I'll keep my eye on him...and hopefully I can keep both eyes by the end of this journey. Trust no one. Signing off for now. Tomorrow I will head to the Dracula orchids.

Phoenix

PARANORMAL INVESTIGATION REPORT:

■ ■ ■ ▬ ▬ ▬

Location: unknown

Date: October 6th

Time: 1:11 am

Notes:

The legend is now clear as day. Cipher and the sea condors don't belong here, their true home is amongst the stars. But the whole...Legion of Zeros and Seyfert the Spinner of Nonsense took over the galaxies. We need to head over to the Dracula orchids...wherever they are. Cipher was resting when I grabbed his book. I figured there would be some sort of clue as to where the haunted orchids are located. Before I could lay my hands on the book Cipher slapped me away with his claws. He stood up. Tall.

As Cipher opened the book, a golden, shimmering paper airplane flew out and took a lap around the cave. The airplane floated delicately but deliberately until it landed perfectly on my hand. I decided to unfold it. The paper airplane was a map! And it looked like it might lead to the Dracula orchids where the hydro-galactic code could be found! Also inside the map was a crushed petal from a Dracula orchid. The delicate pieces of flower morphed into a pink confetti...then that confetti turned into spiders that began crawling up and down my arms. For the first time in a long time, I feared nothing. I shook the spiders off, took my map, my journal, and left the cave. Cipher was two steps behind. Once I get to the Dracula orchids...if I get to the Dracula orchids...I will write back. Wish me luck, whoever is reading this. Sorry if there are crushed spider guts on these pages.

Phoenix

PARANORMAL INVESTIGATION REPORT: . . .

Location: the frozen battlefield

Date: October 7th

Time: unknown

Notes:

The sounds of my desperate panting filled the frigid air. I couldn't stop. We were being chased by an invisible enigma beyond the unknown. I started to fixate on the idea that at any moment I could slip off the ice and fall to my demise. I don't know how we got here and I certainly could not predict how this would end! We were running up a staircase with no end in sight. Encased in ice, the staircase was a mysterious collection of colors laced with shades of white and frigid blue. Its glassy appearance reflected constellations of wild light bursting in every direction. The sky surrounding us was a thick, blinding white haze. Cipher looked exhausted. He was about five stairs behind me, using his claws to help him climb and stay at my pace.

Running! Running Running! I screamed to Cipher to motivate him to keep going! But looking ahead ...there was no end to the staircase. It seemed to lead...nowhere, and the menacing fog was only becoming more suffocating. I also couldn't shake the feeling that if we stopped... we would... die! It felt like we were sprinting for an eternity. Every time I would slow my pace, a frigid chill would send roads of icy goosebumps up and down my body. Clearly, we were on some kind of devilish hamster wheel where giving up meant the end of your life!

My legs began to feel heavy. My heart could not keep up this pace any longer. I stopped. Dead... in... my... tracks. I looked at my feet and let out a shrieking scream. What I saw will haunt me for the rest of my life...even if I only have a few hours remaining! Nestled within the frozen stairs was a collection of eyeballs darting in different directions! Quite literally a STARE-case! The grisly glares were blinking, darting, winking, changing their direction! They were...alive! Some eyes were brown, blue, hazel...neon green?! My own eyes traveled up the staircase to see there were millions of lively eyeballs frozen within. They were watching us the entire time! That's when Cipher took my hand and threw me off the ledge of the STARE-case. My body fell through the haunted smog as if it was weightless. I couldn't see a thing! Then, after blacking out for who knows how long, I woke up in the middle of a frozen lake. Cipher was right beside me.

My mind was torn between believing I was

in a safe place or the place in which I would lose my life. There was a thin layer of twinkling snow covering the peaceful, frozen lake. I began to shift my body as if I was ice skating. The air felt so pure despite the phantom fog still looming above. Sure, we couldn't see our surroundings, but everything we needed to know lay underneath the frozen lake. That's when I realized this place could be the last place I ever see.

Cipher fell to his hands and knees, frantically wiping the light dust of snow from the ice. I decided to join him. My hands began to crystallize from the sharp prick of the frigid snow. This wasn't just any snow. The pain didn't feel cold...it felt scalding hot, as if I was touching molten lava!

I began to use my elbows to sweep the snow away. I still had no idea why we were doing this, but I didn't want to question the legendary beast. Suddenly, I heard Cipher let out a powerful roar that shook the ice beneath me! I ran over to where he was to see him using his vicious claws to pulverize the ice beneath.

As I got closer to Cipher, it was clear as ice. The war had begun. Staring back at us was a legion of skeletons with their ugly skull-faces pressed to the ice glaring back at us. There were millions of them. Their forbidding green eyes scanned mine and locked me in. I couldn't move a muscle... let alone blink! Cipher had created a hole in the ice where one of the skeletons reached his boney hand up. I caught a glimpse of his emerald ring. It was Seyfert, the Spinner of Darkness from the ancient legend.

Suddenly, the entire army rose from the ice, staring Cipher and I down. They started to file into rows. One...after the other...after the other...like some sort of graveyard battalion. Cipher and I remained...frozen.

The horror! My body was locked up as if I were in a frozen straightjacket! The legion slowly moved closer and closer to me. Not once did they break their gaze. I couldn't back up. I couldn't raise my fists. In fact, I couldn't even...remember who I was.

Seyfert was about three inches from my nose when he lifted his skeletal hand to my face. All I could focus on was his menacing eyes and the grisly gem on his finger. He paused. Then, he snapped his fingers. The sound of his bones rubbing together to make a snap ran my blood cold; and with that simple act, Cipher and I were precipitously thrusted into the frozen lake below...only...frozen it was no longer.

The once frozen lake was now a deathly

ocean of thick rushing blood! The red waves came crashing down above us! We were drowning! I could see an eyeball... a spider... worms... and bundles of bones circling in underwater tornados all around me! As I struggled to stay afloat, I squinted my eyes—I could see land in the distance! I knew Cipher and I had to swim there, somehow, in order to survive. Thrashing through the deadly currents, I grabbed Cipher by the claw... or the fin... and pointed toward the land in the distance. Cipher collected himself and linked arms with me (well...arm for me...wing for him) and swam at the speed of sound... almost like we were flying! Before I knew it, we were on solid land. I fell to my knees and coughed up the remains of worms and eyeballs. As my vision started to come back, I saw a field of Dracula orchids in the distance. Cipher and I locked eyes... or...eye. We knew the code to defeat the Spinner of Darkness and restore the sea condors rightful place in the stars lay beyond the Dracula orchids. But before we could think of a strategy on how to get there, we were interrupted by the Legion of Venom standing...right...behind us.

Cipher lunged, his sword-like claws shimmering as he shifted toward the direction of the Legion. He managed to fight off about six of them and push them back into the blood sea. Cipher's blue flame tail was creating a forcefield of fire around him. As he fought the Legion off, I started to run toward the Dracula orchids when a skeleton grabbed me by the ankle and pushed me to the ground. It was Seyfert and his evil ring. I closed my eyes tight and started to punch randomly in the air, hoping my fists would connect with his hideous skull. I didn't want to catch his stare again! Then, Seyfert released his bony grip and let me go. He brought his deathly face close to my ear and whispered, "...how about a game of stare?"

I shot up to my feet and gave him a kick in the jaw, which cracked off his skull and fell to the ground. Seyfert very calmly picked up his detached jaw and snapped it back on his face as if this sort of thing happens all the time! He let out a wicked laugh then lunged for my throat. Narrowly escaping his grip, I ran towards the orchids. As I ran for my life, I kept looking behind me. Seyfert wasn't chasing me; in fact, he was standing still...laughing. I looked beyond his shoulder. Cipher was still at war with the Legion, but one the skeleton soldiers had cast a spell that froze his blue flame tail into a solid block of ice! He was in danger.

After everything we've been through, I couldn't leave Cipher behind! We shared a mission, and we were finally close to cracking the code. I ran over to him despite the danger. I darted right past

Seyfert, who didn't react at all. He just kept...laughing. As I got closer to Cipher, it was clear he was in a lot more trouble than I even realized. With every step I took, the once white fluorescent sky became increasingly dark and grim with the black of night. I had to get to Cipher before nightfall. It seemed like the faster I ran and the closer I thought I got, somehow everything became farther and farther away!

A loud explosion knocked me off my feet. The sound ripped through the atmosphere. As I looked around, it seemed like everybody, including the Legion, fell to the ground like boney dominos from beyond the crypt! I looked up to see that the sky was illuminated by beautiful neon fireworks! I have never seen anything as beautiful in my entire life! Like exploding swords, the phantom fireworks cut through the darkness, restoring my faith that I was going to get out of here. I stood up. The light from the fireworks revealed the legend. I could see the metallic fins of the sea condors glistening like shooting starlight reflected on their fins of blades. Swimming above me was an entire legion of sea condors painting their own constellations in the sky above! Suddenly, the hundreds of mythical beasts plunged their bodies onto the Legion of Venom below. The sounds of bones clashing with metallic fins will haunt my memory for eternity, but I had to brave the hydro-galactic war. This is what I came for!

Right before my very eyes, a great battle between the stars and the sea broke out. Fireworks, bioluminescent waves and the reflection of bones filled the air! Then, a brilliant inferno of blazing blue caught my eye. It was Cipher.

Dodging the deathly stares from the skeleton army, I made my way to Cipher, who was in deep trouble! Seyfert had Cipher by the throat, and I could see the evil emerald ring reflecting in Seyfert's eye. In the midst of the sea condors pulverizing the skeletons, I grabbed a bone from the ground and swiftly knocked Seyfert's head off his shoulders. With the powerful fire of his tail, Cipher illuminated the battlefield and began to roar! In an instant, the massive flock of sea condors returned to the waters. What remained? A sinister graveyard of skeleton bones. Did we just win the war? Everything was very still for about a minute before each and every skeleton began to shift around and move. Are they coming back to life? The remains of the Legion were now looking for their missing pieces as they began to reassemble themselves! Cipher abruptly grabbed and dragged me to the sea. As I slipped below the bloody waters, I felt the pain of sharp claws digging into my shoulders!

Every time I tried to come up for air, my head was pushed down deeper and deeper. I began to realize...Cipher was...drowning me.

I tried to fight back when suddenly I felt an enormous swing from below the depths. The force of the current created a wave that sent my body flying at supersonic speed!

As I soared against my will, my eyes could make out a little bit of my surroundings. Visions of metallic gold and crimson red became clear! I was in the presence of a sea condor...but not just any...it was Sansu. I instantly knew it due to his enormous eye—some say he had a bigger eye than the rest of the pod because he has seen more in his life than most others.

Sansu's giant wing created an air bubble that locked me in its clutches. The warm presence of air gave me the courage to take a breath! It worked; I was actually breathing underwater. The legendary beast had created an air pocket for me to rest in.

Before I knew it, my time with Sansu came to an end. The great monster swiped his powerful wing one last time, sending me on an underwater elevator of mystery once again. After blacking out again, I woke up on dry land. But this time, I was...dinner.

I could feel tiny razor teeth digging into my arms and legs. A molten burn overtook my skin and the veins on my arms began to swell. I was being eaten alive...by the orchids...the Dracula orchids. I lept to my feet and began to kick at the carnivorous plants, hoping I wouldn't lose an arm or a leg in the process! These plants were huge! And just when I thought things couldn't get worse, Cipher appeared out of nowhere! I sprung into a defensive stance, preparing to face the beast who just tried to drown me in the blood ocean of doom! But instead of attacking me, Cipher slowly began to claw at the plants, paving a safe path for us to walk on. Where were we going? Cipher seemed to know. I had no choice but to follow, but I kept a safe distance from him at all times just in case he flipped a switch. Who knows when he would snap again?

Night had fallen...but this was not just any night. I have never seen the sky such a deep shade of black. Not one single star, nebula, or planet could be seen. There was not a single hopeful shimmer of light to guide us. We were staring into a blank cosmic abyss...not a sky. The only shimmer of light we had was the glow of Cipher's eye.

We came to an abrupt stop. Cipher seemed

to hesitate a bit as he opened the ancient mythical book and turned to a random page. As he held the open page, a warm golden light filled the air and cut through the black sky. Dancing shimmering letters began to appear in the sky before forming a message:

"Pick the flower with the fewest thorns."

Time to pick a flower...back to the bloodthirsty orchids! The flower's leaves felt thick and durable, almost like leather! The pink and orange hues of the plant were vibrant and neon! The green stem seemed as strong as the trunk of a mighty tree that had been in this exact spot since the dawning of time. Its roots seemed permanently sewn into the earth. Never have I ever seen such a brilliant looking plant. As I looked closer, I could see that the plant even had a face...a real face! The orchid's mouth had long fangs and a huge tongue! And, sure enough...the Dracula orchid had only...one eye! Next to the plant were two smaller, shriveled and shrunken flowers that looked as if they had weathered every single storm that ever happened. The decaying plants were encased in the thick white webbing of spiders that have come and gone through the centuries. The most garish thing about these orchids? Each one had razor blade thorns covering almost every inch of its stem!

I decided to refocus on the mission at hand. I had to pluck the Dracula orchid with the fewest thorns...so I did exactly that. I wrapped my hand around the stem that did not have any thorns and pulled with all my might! As the plant left the dirt, an endless trail of roots emerged with it. Since when do flowers have such long roots? I kept tugging and tugging until I found myself ten feet away from where the flower once stood! I began to pull on the roots to get the flower free, but I felt a force as though the flower was getting pulled back to the ground! Was I playing tug-of-war with someone or...something... who lived underground? Cipher and I joined forces and continued to tug at the plant. It was at that exact moment that the sky fell.

That's right! I said it! The sky fell... well... maybe a few thousand feet closer to us! It was as if someone wanted us to see the galaxies just a little bit closer. Suddenly, Cipher took out his mysterious spray can once again. He urgently began to spray the black night sky until the mist blinded our eyes and filled our lungs. Once the fog settled, we could see red neon numbers right where the sky should have been:

19,5,22,5,14———16,5,20,1,12,9

I had no clue what this meant and it didn't

seem like Cipher knew much either. Perhaps this was the ancient code that could defeat Seyfert and the Legion of Venom? Cipher began to pace nervously. Then he grabbed me by my arms and pulled me close. I was face-to-face with his cyclops eye! Every time I would try to pull away, he made sure to focus my attention to his eyes. He began to blink wildly. The moment was interrupted by a little, sparkling paper airplane that was wisping around my head. Cipher and I both looked up at the aircraft! I grabbed it and started to unravel its wings. Inside the paper airplane was a lightning bug shining a light on the word "count." I cracked the code! It all started to make sense! Cipher wanted me to count the number of times he blinked.

I secured my eye contact with the beast and told him to start.

The first time he blinked 19 times then he clapped and blinked 5 times. He blinked 22 times, then clapped 5 more. He blinked 14 more times. I knelt down and recorded the number of blinks with my finger in the dirt. He then blinked 16 times, clapped 5 more times, made 20 more blinks, clapped another single clap, blinked 12 times and 19 times. These were the numbers in the stars. Cipher knelt down next to me and wrote a message in the dirt. It said "letters."

I decided to write the alphabet out on the dirt and number of the letters. The letter

A went with the number 1, the letter B went with the number 2, and so on. I would then put letters to the number codes. 19,5,22,5,14——16,5,20,1,12,19 spelled out, "seven petals."

Cipher grabbed the phantom tug-of-war orchid from before and started to pluck seven petals from its head. Suddenly, the plant grew teeth and began to snap and growl at Cipher who dodged its vicious teeth with every pluck.

Cipher quickly sat up and the fur on his back began to rise. It was as if every hair on his body started to point to the sky. He was sensing danger. The great beast whipped his tail around and shot a blue flame in the distance for some light. The blue blaze showed Seyfert and his green ring on the other end of the Dracula orchid root. He was the one playing tug-of-war!

We were out of time. Cipher handed me the petals and shot a flame to the sky once again. Was he trying to summon someone? Suddenly, an enormous skeleton in a phantom cloak appeared as a grimacing constellation above! He was a grim collection of stars with a wicked looking face. I don't know what came over me, but I decided to throw the seven petals as hard as I could at the galactic phantom! One petal floated gently in the air before it lightly rested in the palm of my hand.

I stopped and stared at it. Suddenly, the petal started to move and shake! A flash appeared and almost knocked me off my feet. In an instant, the little petal became a mighty steel sword!

The sky began to pour monsoons of rain upon us. I could see herds of sea condors jolting out of the sea and swimming into the stars, while pieces of skeletons fell from the sky and into the sea! Were the sea condors migrating back home? Then, Seyfert the Spinner of Darkness appeared right in front of me! I could see the galactic phantom in the sky right behind Seyfert. Both phantoms began to open their viscous mouths at the same time. Seyfert revealed his wicked werewolf-like fangs drenched in sticky spit and...phantom venom! I threw the last petal into the Spinner of Darkness's mouth, causing him to choke! His hand and ring blasted off his body in a cosmic explosion that caused an earthquake! The ring shot into the sky like an emerald asteroid on a celestial mission. Turns out, it was. Do you want to know where his ring went? Take a look at the night sky tonight! Where do you think the North Star came from?

Eventually, Seyfert caught his breath and lunged at me once more. But Cipher jumped in front of me like a shield! The last moment I fully remember was Cipher opening up his book and flipping some sort of switch hidden within the pages.

I have to rush this report; I'm not sure how much time is left. But once Cipher flipped the switch, a phantom red light erased everything and everyone around us. It was just me and Seyfert. Seyfert's evil hand grabbed mine and that's when the switch w. e. N. T. Off.

THE PHANTOM'S TEA TABLE: BEHIND THE TEA!

WISE WORDS FROM THE AUTHOR... IF YOU DARE

Hello there Phan-dom,

Sorry…did I switch something off by accident? I'm so glad I tended to my Dracula orchids! They made for a chilling tale, right? Well, you made it out of the silent circus, defeated the two-face arcade, and somehow survived the stare. I'm *monstrously* impressed! See what I did there? You know, every time I look up at the stars, I'm going to think about Seyfert and his Legion of Venom. But I'm also going to think about the sea condors! Sometimes in life, you're going to meet people who reveal themselves over time. Maybe they start out nice to you and then end up as your worst nightmare! That's what happened in *Two Face Arcade*, but *The Stare* shows you that sometimes people are in fact who they've always seemed to be…and that might not always be a good thing.

At one point, you might find yourself in the midst of a Legion of Venom. Their glares and stares are going to try to silence or intimidate you into becoming something you're not. Maybe their stares will silence you? Please shine brighter than every star in the sky…like the sea condors! Let the toxic villains watch you from below! Their stares have no power amongst the stars! I once had my own brush with a Legion of Venom of sorts. It was tough, but I made it out stronger than ever! Anyhow, I have to figure out how to fix this switch. Maybe you can help me? We need to see what happened to Phoenix, Cipher, and the sea condors. I think we should relocate. We need a change in scenery. What do you say? Follow me to the next adventure?

Sending you cheers and a side of fear,
Danica Mendez

THE PHANTOM CODE CHALLENGE!

When Phoenix had to work with codes, I'm pretty willing to bet secret spies and special agents came to your mind! What if I told you there is a secret code you can learn, and it was a major part of American history?! Have you ever heard of Morse code? It's been around since the 1800s!

Morse code is used to send telegraphic messages using rhythm. Imagine communicating through the simple taps of your finger. Morse code is made up of dots and dashes to show different letters and numbers! When messages are sent by Morse code, dots are short taps and dashes are longer ones. Let's take a look at the diagram below!

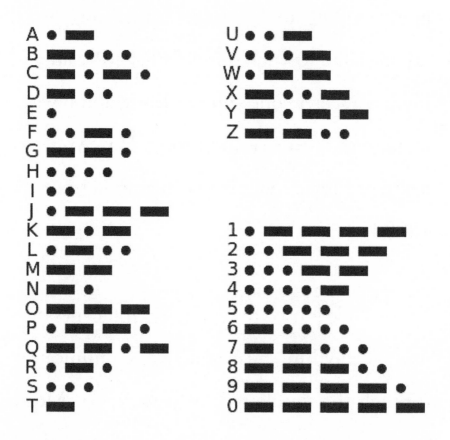

Remember, imagine the dots as short taps and

the dashes as longer taps.

Let's see if you can decipher the following message to reveal the title of the next Phantom's Tea book! Tap it out!

—— ——

·

———

· ——— ·

——— ——— ———

· ——— ——— ·

—— —— ——

· —— · ·

· ·

· · ·

· · ·

· — —

· ·

— —

— — · — — ·

· · · ·

Something tells me this is not the last you will see of Phoenix and Cipher. In fact, they wanted me to give you this message!

· · · ·

·

· — — · ·

· — — ·

— — —

·

Made in United States
North Haven, CT
05 July 2023

38557598R00071